I0655197

Craig Babcock's
Poems & Short Stories

2022

Quantum
Craig Babcock's Poems & Short Stories

Copyright © 2022 Craig Babcock
All Rights Reserved

First American Edition

ISBN 978-0-578-32795-2

Cover art and book design by Helen Kaar

Without limiting the rights under copyright above, no part of this publication may be reproduced, stored, or introduced into a retrieval system, or transmitted in any form, or by any means (electronically, mechanically, photocopying, recording, or otherwise) without the proper prior written permission of the copyright owner, except in the case of brief quotations embodied in critical articles and reviews.

Published by JCB Words on Paper
Rockaway Township, NJ

*For my wife Margaret,
and our sons
Frederick Scott and Evan Kendall*

Contents

Poems

Stories

Poems

Free Spirit

I suppose that the proper term for me is water spirit.
I have always been just fine with faery. After all, with over
two thousand solar cycles I am rather used to it.
Previously the biggest challenge in my existence
was the trip from my Irish home to the New World in the
belly of a ship.

Now, here I am at home in an artesian spring in
Ironia, New Jersey. My major concern remains where are
the other faeries? Sorry, water spirits. Also, not too long ago
several big dark green trucks with men in orange vests came
here and put up a metal fence all around and over my abode.
Just what is a DPW?

No more are there offerings of flowers, bread, cheese,
and wine. No longer are there the happy sounds of people
big and small seeking favors, blessings, or just a drink of
fresh spring water. No one is here to properly present the
respectful libation of some small amount of what is taken,
poured back to the god. Hello, that would be me!

It has taken me a long time to understand the words coming
from these New World people, but I get it. Whatever
"Not Potable" and "Contaminated" are, they are not good
words. To draw attention, I have tried being a young
cottontail, a blue-spotted salamander, a yellow Hammond
wildflower in full bloom, and a crystal of unusual beauty.
All to no avail.

If you get this message, I plead with you, please come with
a watertight container, stout bolt cutters, and liberate me. I
admit that I am not as influential as in times past, but
especially if you live near water, I can still do you
some good.

Fall Leaf

Mother tree release my dried out aged self,
push me out into the abyss below.
Breeze take me. Moving air support me.
Propel me in my gentle plunge.
Draw me to you, constant earthly pull.
Here I come my brothers
as I free fall to join you.
Glorious exhilarating frightening freedom.
Plummet, pirouette, swoop,
flutter, dip, glide.
As I was one with us all,
in greenness and sunlight,
accept me now as I am,
just like you, all golden rust red,
together headed into dark dampness.
My consciousness further melds
within the greater oaken community.
In days to come, like you,
I will blend into the earth,
becoming one with
fungi and sustaining roots,
gathered and embraced.

Bird Feeder, Bird Feeder

Madam Bird Feeder come fill me up.
We attend to those who otherwise stay distant.
They empty me one seed at a time,
fly off away, swoop, swoop.
Take one to the best shucking place,
or hide-save one for winter,
or open-devour one right here, now.
Defend me from the thief
furry acrobat descender.
Witness a sparrow hoard invasion
squabbling, scattering my contents
to the ground below where
chipmunks and squirrels roam,
scavenging edible bits that rain from above.
A red cardinal delicately feeds his mate.
Nuthatches walk upside down, down
to the lowest hole where the best seeds hide.
Fat starving offspring franticly beg their mothers
Feed me! Feed me! Feed me!
Bug eaters choose the easy feed of seed.
Four or five kinds of woodpeckers come and go,
dominant by size, largest red head reigns supreme.
Some flit in, flit out, gone in a second.
Chic-a-dee. Chic-a-dee-dee.
Madam Bird Feeder lower me,
clean me, fill me up again.
As you raise me up to the anxious many
those that just cannot resist, ride along,
grabbing a seed as I ascend to station.
Together we are the sustaining magnet.
Bird Feeder, Bird Feeder.

Message in a Bottle

Extraterrestrial life
welcome at this location.
An invitation
to the Universe,
on behalf of a
planet called Earth.
Open House.
Come as you are.
No restrictions.
Reservations not required.
All beings welcome.
Mostly water
on the outside.
Enveloped in gases,
an iron nickel core.
Sixth major surface
change underway.
Look for the stunning
blue ball, white accents,
in near orbit
a cratered moon.
Third out from the speckled
yellow dwarf star,
close to the edge of
a spiral galaxy.

Princess Jenny

One wild turkey hen
standing midship atop
an inverted canoe,
dominates the Old Town
sixteen-footer and all around.
Family gathers beneath
to witness her beauty
and courage. Slow half
pirouette, wings outstretched,
then tucked. Display over,
she descends to the forest floor.
In just moments,
the flock disappears,
as turkeys do.

Proper Attire

Usually, I only wear
my grandmother's necklace to grand events,
my new waterproof boots to hike on park trails,
my black stiletto pumps to elegant dinners,
easy-casual-nice to the hairdressers,
my baseball hat to the ballpark,
my designer tennis shoes to play doubles.

Usually, I only wear
my silk scarf and butterfly pin to book club,
my better wool sweater to County Library,
my championship jersey to pub game night,
a pretty seasonal dress to play duplicate bridge,
my over-the-shoulder tote bag to shop at the Mall,
my pink durag to work out at the gym.

Usually, I only wear
my extra-large hoodie to walk in the neighborhood,
my crocheted ivory shawl to church,
my blue jeans and painting shirt to do yardwork,
a fancy blouse to school-buddies brunch,
my London trench coat to visit my partner's mother,
my tailored pant suit to work on staff meeting days.

Now, in Covid lockdown,
I only wear
my not-worn-more-than-a-week
sweats, all day, every day.

Runs in the Family

The father was hair disadvantaged.
>   Everyone grieved for his loss.

The mother was too short for her weight.
>   The kids showed signs of dessert deprivation.

The sister was fashion disabled.
>   Gal's Deal Shed sent her frequent shopper coupons.

The brother was crime enabled.
>   Postal patrons nationwide knew his rap sheet.

The grandfathers were manners impaired.
>   Waitresses for miles around despaired.

The grandmothers were sweetness overflowing.
>   Young mothers came away sticky.

The uncles were fault free and knew Right.
>   Anyone with a problem showed great restraint.

The aunts were the information superhighway.
>   Bystanders knew much more than they cared.

Envied, generation after generation, the Family
>   cheerfully bore the benefits of perfect teeth.

Got it. [tap finger to forehead] Right here!

The key. The exact amount. The password.
The proper code. What should come next.
How to fasten it. How to unlock it.
How to print. How I made it work before.
The reason I came up here. Which two keys
to press simultaneously. Where I am now.
I know I have seen it. It is in a specific place.
The way to put it together that includes part D.
I carefully put it in my special contact list,
giving it a secret name, so I would remember.
What she said that was so so funny.
Whether the phone number ends in 38 or 83.
Where I always keep it. The last time I used it.
What is so important that I must do it right now.
It'll come to me, in a minute.

What?

Tell me no "truth" for
I dwell in my mighty self.
My reality is reality.
I am the lawful power.
I was chosen to be what I am.
I got here by being me.
You know me.
My right is right.
I am the boss, the judge,
the proclaimer of what is,
as seen on TV.
My now is the now for all.
I speak. What I say is.
What I say goes.
If I say it more than once,
that is how you know it is true.
Out there, there are many
many lies, many lies, much fakery,
even extremist perversion,
not my reality.
Listen to me, believe me, follow me,
be loyal to greatness.
I am the path, the way, all you need.
Beware, be vigilant, there are many
nasty nasty plots against me.
I am the answer. I have done
a great job, a spectacular job,
none better ever in all of history.
What?

4 Monkey Shtick

ancient name: Mi-zara
you can call me Bob
see no evil – your choice
get the sunglasses pair, one black & one mirror
at the 4 Monkey Shtick gift shop
or seek and be present to natural beauty.

ancient name: Cica-zara
you can call me Jim
hear no evil – your choice
get the washable ear plugs & case
at the 4 Monkey Shtick gift shop
or seek and be present to pleasing sound.

ancient name: Yues-zara
you can call me Bill
speak no evil – your choice
get the vow-of-silence necklace & bracelet set
at the 4 Monkey Shtick gift shop
or seek and be present to the words of truth and love.

ancient name: Sed-zara
you can call me Sue
do no evil – your choice
get the full assortment & the comfy stool
at the 4 Monkey Shtick gift shop
or seek and be present to compassion and generosity.

Snow Fairies

Snow Fairies may be anywhere there is snow. However, since they can move under the mantle of snow, without disturbing the surface, their presence is rarely observed.

On the occasion that they are above the snow they can choose to blend in by matching the array of whites and blues as expressed in the frozen water around them.

Should you come across one out in the open, where movement might have given it away, you can address it, respectfully. Flattery helps. Cautious requests, this-for-that deals, help in making things better or worse are possible, at a price.

Be wary of the twinkling eye, the too-good-to-be-true offer, and excessive enthusiasm. A gleeful dance is not a good sign. These ethereal magical beings have no natural enemies and remain self-possessed and fiercely independent.

Rest assured that creatures who eat snow are not intentionally ingesting snow fairies, although, as tiny and as invisible as they can be, this may, regrettably, happen from time to time.

Spirits of the Snow, as they are sometimes called, remain enticingly beautiful, elusive, and untrustworthy. Please report verifiable sightings to The Institute of the Unproven, dot org, Fairies Division.

Djembe Queen
Drum of My Life

I take you from your case,
place you in your stand,
just the way I like you.

Before we begin,
with affection I caress
your smooth top surface,
then a quick medley, saying,
Wake up. We are here.

At your very center,
I thump you strong and exact
in the very spot that produces
the bass that resonates deep
in the heart of each listener.
The bottom. The foundation.
The sustain of what is to follow.

As I play you,
creating what is in my head,
I delight in the amazing range
of sound we produce.
I am careful to leave space,
emptiness, for breath, contrast,
and the music of others.

I give import to the downbeat,
adding expressive comment.
On rare occasion
I lean on my elbow,
hard into your middle,
letting up slowly,
as I stroke you to vary the pitch.

In the moment,
I am filled with joy,
listening fully present,
holding it all together.
Supporting, filling out,
adding accent and counterpoint,
mirroring or reversing phrases,
moving listeners to the dance within.

Each time we play I gladly
give you some of myself.
We contain, store, and build on
our mutual experience. Together
we have accumulated soul.

Finished for now,
with love I rub
your smooth surface
saying, Thank you,
my Djembe Queen.

Antique Wheels

Still on the road
after all these years.

Passed my annual checkup,
everything functional and well.
Not like last year when I
had to have my right suspension
totally replaced with
custom titanium steel.

Previously losing power,
lacking acceleration,
diagnostics revealed that
a valve had gone bad.
Mandatory major engine
surgery, with rebuilding,
… days in the shop.

Threatening shut down,
gunk grew inside me.
Treatments applied over
months eliminated it all.
Saved me. Preserved me.

Nine fuel additivies
help me run smooth.

Dings, scratches, blemishes
used to annoy me no end.
Now they are just accents.
Been a long, long time since
I was shiny and eye catching.

Every inspection cycle I wish
I had been built supercharged.
This passes because I know
what really matters is that
each day I start easy and
just keep rolling along.

Cicada Cicada

Waiting, deep
among the tree roots,
at last the urgent call,
the Big Dance is now!

Rise up, ascend,
break out into the air sea.
Scramble up high,
latch on, crack open.
Emerge transformed with
glorious lacey wings.

Aching for my one special lady,
fly to the everyman tree.
Sing her unique love song,
rattle-buzz, buzz-rattle.
She hears, comes to me,
with sparkling big red eyes.
We hug, touch, feel, fondle,
make the ultimate embrace.

Full of joy, spent, complete.
Soon to meld with
my brothers and sisters
at the end of life,
descending to become
one with our
brown Earth home.

For Safety's Sake

I advocate the selective negation
of the force of Gravity to be
waved in moments of peril,
                    so that:

fallen airplanes float inches off the ground,
discharged bullets rise harmlessly into space,
shaken buildings pause significantly before collapse,
and dropped car keys
                    hover just above sewer grates.

I champion the occasional disruption
of Reality to be held at bay
in the face of stupidity,
                    so that:

anger-driven tongues wag without sound,
macho-leaden feet find the brake
when accelerator-bound, hate-blinded eyes
suddenly see only fellow human beings,
and bare hands with pick-up-hot-pan intent,
                    do a little dance.

Summer Shore Romance

She walked in a vegan
save-the-timber wolves way,
earnest beyond question,
each step one more
towards a better world.

Uniformed in bandana bound tresses,
long sleeved unbleached cotton top,
modest-in-length cuffed jean shorts,
her pale bipedal motion propels
roll-topped bobbie-sock-filled white Keds.

Her oblivion is total to
the rhythm of waves, clear blue sky,
the unblemished white sand beach
expansive at low tide.

Her considerable extra-large
sunglasses-filtered attention
remains riveted on a hard bound
subscriber-only Harlequin novel
titled, *Rebecca's Prince Has Come!*

Freethinker Inner Peace

Present in the moment, happy to be stardust,
a planetary air recycler, a water being.
Accepting complexity, impermanence, open to
interdependence, relationship with all.
Intentionally broadening perception, both out and in.
Listening to my heartbeat, feeling my pulse,
my lungs working. Marveling in my mostly
automatic body. Home to life and change.
Feeling, hearing, seeing, tasting,
at heart so like my fellow humans.
Unburdened by belief, dogma, and Right ways,
able to laugh at uncontrollable mind, seek stillness.
Imagining standing, surrounded by microbes
and fungi, being a common community of atoms,
one with all in this moment.

One Ardent Cricket
On
The Marginal Way

Thank you, Josiah Chase, and
people of Ogunquit Maine for
free to all, public access,
to one and a quarter mile of
wild North Atlantic coast.

Vast open ocean to the horizon,
right before you incoming waves
break over exposed bedrock,
rolling dark aqua marine transforms
into crashing cascading pure white,
smells of seaweed and salt water,
sounds like constant pulsing wind.

Pause, take time to witness
nine-to-eleven-foot tidal change,
while safely above, at the edge of
the sea's uncaring restless power.

A male cricket, seeking a mate,
vigorously rubs his wings together
in persistent hopeful driven necessity,
solid ancient cliff, ocean, blue skies,
one penetrating sound perseveres,
oblivious to location.

Common Turkey Vulture

Each morning with
my wings spread wide
I stand still and
greet the warming sun.
Only when I am ready
do I take flight.

Then I soar, circle,
glide, ride the air.
From above I can see
and smell my wildlife buffet.

No need to hurry,
my food lies still.
I cannot grab and go
and must eat where
the meal is served.

Mostly, I share
with friends and
they with me.
I only squabble
when I do not
get my share.

I am gifted with
rot in my gut.
I am what I eat.

At sunset I join others
in the large roost tree,
comforted to be together,
resting for the new day to come.

Old New Love

In this moment you are here.
In the same moment I am here.
Together we are vibrant, alive.

As we age, a growing number of
family, friends, and acquaintances
have gone beyond, passed away,
been gathered to their ancestors,
present only in our hearts and minds.

Here, now, pay attention,
be available, considerate,
affectionate, enjoy differences,
be pleasing and pleased.

Avoid unintended insult.
Shun automatic defense.
See, hear, sense each other.
Make space for one and two.
Give in to the irrational.

Embrace passion, enjoy touch,
hug with joy, communicate
mind to mind, body to body.
Let in happiness.

May it be so.

Stories

My Big Break

A last-minute booking came in on just ten days' notice. As a solo mime, sometimes I just had to take whatever work came along. The sponsor wanted two back-to-back one hour and a half performance workshops for elementary age children. That was much longer than I normally worked for this age group. My first thought was this is just not possible. However, the money was very good and very needed. So, I told my agent that I would make it work.

As I was escorted by the principal from the school office to the all-purpose room she said, "By the way, someone from Alvin Ailey is coming to see you."

"They are?" I said in surprise.

Stopping in her tracks she stated firmly, "Well, if they do not have your permission, I will simply tell them 'No' when they arrive."

"No. No, I am sure it is okay. They must have cleared it with my agent," I said, shocked that someone could so easily alter the course of my future success. Tell them no, indeed! I envisioned the lights slowly dimming on the expansive Lincoln Center stage. A hush of anticipation sweeping over the formally attired, sold-out house. The applause beginning as the first dancers enter from the wings and surging to a deafening roar as I walk on bathed in a follow spot. No. Indeed!

As I warmed up, I eagerly contemplated the possibilities. Reluctantly I was forced to admit that I could not fathom why anyone from the Alvin Ailey Dance Company would come to see me perform. Surely, they do not really want a person of my age, weight, and color to perform with all those perfect, young, elegant black dancers. Maybe they want someone to teach the company some specific skills that I have to offer. I would just have to wait and see.

I kept a sharp eye out, but I did not see anyone who looked as if they were from Alvin Ailey, nor did anyone come up and speak to me before the first performance was to start.

Just as I took the stage, moving to stage center, standing very still, commanding attention, I saw a beautiful, mature, black woman enter the back of the hall. She was very self-possessed. The lady had perfect posture and was quietly graceful. I saw the principal speak to her.

She-who-was-to-establish-my-presence-in-the-New-York-City-market sat down in the back row. I was surprised how self-conscious her being there made me feel. I struggled to not significantly extend moments, not to think see this, this is why you should hire me – for whatever it is.

Thankfully, the performance went very well, despite its long running time. There was very little additional workshop as I incorporated participation into the show with exercises using the whole audience right where they were. At one point, in a joking way, I asked the ladies in the back who were not participating, which included the woman from Alvin Ailey, to join in. "My future" laughed as she joined in and flashed a smile of pure morning sunshine.

Rising from my last bow, full of expectation, I looked to the back of the house, only to find she was gone. Not one word. I went to get my silenced cell phone from my gig bag and realized I did not have time to call my agent because the second audience was filing in.

After the second show and necessary stage edge conversations with audience members, I called my agent. Knowing that he would recognize my voice, I skipped the normal pleasantries and blurted out, "Do you know anything about someone from the Alvin Ailey Dance Company coming to see me perform this afternoon?"

Slowly he said, "No," sounding puzzled.

"Well, a beautiful lady from the Alvin Ailey Dance Company was here to see me but she did not talk to me before or after the performance. The only way she could have known about my performing here, since it was such a last-minute booking, is from you."

With the experience of years in the business, evident by the gentle understanding carried in his voice, the person actually responsible for my future said, "Well, I think I sent invitations to all the nearby schools. If I remember correctly, one of them is the Alvin Ailey Elementary School."

Flock Talk

Beatrice: Harriot said that Wilma said that Louise is near done laying. She is less than one a day.

Louise: Well, I don't know why Wilma is anyone to talk. If hers get any smaller she will have to go live with the quail.

Natalie: Excuse me dear but there is a tasty grasshopper right behind you.

Wilma: Beatrice says she is going for a record. She is trying for one two in a day.

Natalie: I heard that there are more numbers than one two. But I don't get it. One two is good enough for me.

Wilma: Red lady bugs are my favorite!

Martha: I like spiders!

Mildred: I ate a caterpillar yesterday. It was yucky, tickled all the way down.

Beatrice: Yesterday Mildred shouted out like a rooster, I'm organic. What ever that is. I'm organic.

Natalie: If she is organic aren't we all?

Louise: She just wants to be Number One Hen.

Harriot: Can you imagine Mildred Number One Hen?

Beatrice: Mildred, Mildred someone fouled my roost!

Louise: And she is going to do something about it? I think not.

Mildred: Martha you laid your egg in my nest again.

Martha: They are all the same to me.

Louise: I hope we have Bumper Buffet again soon.

Harriot: What is Bumper Buffet?

Natalie: That's right Harriot, you weren't there.

Louise: Bumper Buffet is when we get out into the parking lot and feast on squashed bugs on the front of cars.

Wilma: Sounds yucky!

Martha: Too intense!

Mildred: I like some greens with my bugs.

Harriot: Picky, picky, picky.

Louise: You would like it if you tried it.

Wilma: Have you ever had a rooster?

Louise: Here we go again!

Harriot: Roosters love this little dance.

Natalie: Shake it Harriot!

Harriot: Where do our eggs go? We lay them, then go out to eat and play, come back and they are gone.

Beatrice: Have any of you raised a brood?

Martha: What's a brood?

Natalie: Fresh alfalfa is the best.

Louise: Young timothy is my favorite.

Harriot: I'll take oat or flax sprouts any day.

Natalie: As long as it's green and fresh, it's for me.

Martha: Where did Gladys go? She was here and now she is not.

Mildred: What does out to pasture mean?

Beatrice: Isn't that where we are?

Natalie: I don't know, and I don't want to dwell on it.

Harriot: I really like it here.

Wilma: Red lady bugs are my favorite.

Martha: I like spiders.

Louise: Let's go by the flowers and eat some butterflies.

Strong Rope

No easy rescue this one, Elma thought as her ambulance came to a stop. The delivery van, crumpled at the corners, had rolled at least once, and was miraculously suspended over the abyss, held back by a few mangled bushes and a distorted guard rail. Heightening the danger, the air was pungent with gasoline fumes.

"Rescue One, Rescue One, what is your location?" She broadcast over the general emergency band, calling immediately for the best help. Earlier they had heard Rescue One out on a traffic accident. They had not heard them radio return-to-quarters and Elma hoped to get them to respond as soon as possible. But there was no response.

"Get a rope on that back bumper. Tie it off to our front hitch," she told the rookie driver, unable to recall his name. She thought to herself, I hope he knows where the rope is and can tie a decent knot. I hope to hell the rope is there. Trying to recall if it had been replaced after last Sunday's ladders drill.

"Headquarters, Ambulance 310. We have a van over the edge on Mountain View Road. Headquarters, Ambulance 310." She stopped and swore as all she got was static. Oh no. We must be in a dead spot or out of range.

It was just the two of them, returning from a one-way transport of a cancer patient to a bigger hospital. Coming back over the mountain from Our Lady of Mercy Hospital in Stewartsville, they had both noticed the skid marks just before they came upon the wreck.

"No flares! No flares!" she yelled. Catching what's-his-name just in time – unlit flares in hand.

He nodded, understanding, gesturing BOOM with his arms. He shouted back, "I don't think anyone is in there. There was no answer when I checked."

Right, she thought. The van was just out for a little jaunt on its own. Where do they get these people?

"Keep trying to reach Headquarters and have them dispatch Rescue One and an engine," she ordered, stepping over the taut rope, heading for the van. "See if anyone was thrown clear."

As she approached, she was aware of the creaking of stressed metal and the slow crunch of compressed gravel. If I can just reach the handle of the side door. If it is unlocked and not jammed. I might be able to pull it open and gain access. Got it, aided in her effort as the van slowly slid another few inches over the edge and stopped. "Hey!"she yelled. "Did you set the damn break? Is the rig in park?"

I should get the hell out of here, she thought in near panic. To her surprise, the van's front seats were empty, and the windshield was blown out. I'll be damned. He's right. Whoever was in here must have been thrown clear. Not over the cliff, I hope.

She was just turning away when amidst the sounds of snapping branches, crunching gravel, and sliding metal she suddenly realized that the soft and unmistakable whimper she was hearing was a baby!

Pushing aside a box that was angled against the back of the driver's seat Elma discovered a baby, safely cocooned in a car seat, held in place by a rear passenger seatbelt. As she freed and grasped the baby, she felt the van again start to slide and a strong hand grab her by the back of her pants. Pulled away, she had a glimpse of open space below as the van slowly slid away. She scrambled and was yanked back up, onto the road.

Baby firmly in her arms, Elma was persistently pulled up the road, away from the edge. She got to see the ambulance follow the van over the cliff with all its emergency lights still flashing. She thought, it must be in neutral, because if it was in park, not all the lights would be on.

Released from the firm grip of her partner she turned around to face him. She read his name on his coat. Elma looked him straight in the eyes and said, "Thanks Bob."

Bob reached out and took the baby form Elma saying, "There is a lady over here, just coming around, who will be very glad to see this." Starting across the road to where the stunned mother was sitting, he looked back at Elma and said, "Strong rope."

One Elephant

Someone…please…help…me. I do not want to be here. I really do not want to go out there before all those eyes. It will be too bright and too loud. I am afraid. Everywhere enemies will stare at me. A many-many flock of death-bringers perch all around. I will be fixed in their sight. From the earth, up high into the air above, tiny white eyes will point their dark spots into my heart. I will be made to walk around before them. I must hide, run away. I want to go home to my right-smelling green place, to the safety of my family. Help.

I barely feel food-bringer's small front foot on my leg. With his other front foot he rubs my chin. It feels good, comforts me. He makes soft noises. Food-bringer is all right, safe. Tonight, he has purple feathers coming out of his head. He has a shiny smooth yellow skin. I still know him. He smells the same. How does he change skin? Why be yellow? I am grey, wrinkled, and look very good all the time.

Food-bringer climbs up my side and sits on my neck. He puts his back legs down behind my ears. Go, he will say. Turn this way. Turn that way. Stop. He will ask me to do strange moves. Then he will bring me food and wet me all over.

I hear the big man-voice bellowing. Now there are many squeaky toots and sharp bangs, all jumbled up, not saying anything. Soon food-bringer with his feet will say Go. It is night. I should stay here in the darkness. I…Go…

As I step into bright daylight many joyful sounds fill my ears and flood my head. I walk slow and straight. I see many little hunters. Young. I see their teeth and hear their happy noise. I am still alive.

My skin prickles to be here. Food-bringer speaks to me. I go to the middle of the valley. Everyone looks at me. I lift my front feet up high off the earth. I hold my head up high. On my own I call out. Hey look! I am here! The pink and brown faced flock all make a big noise with their front feet and with their voices. Again, I wish my sisters and my mother and my grandmother could see me keep these dangerous strange-skinned animals away by standing as they do, on my back feet. I wish my mom could see how I make them all forget to hurt me and make them happy. My sisters would never believe me unless they saw me do it. My family would be startled to see me put my tail end on a big ball. What would they think if they saw me let a yellow hunter with purple feathers coming out of his head stand on my nose? I call real loud, Hey look! I am here! Now I go to eat and to get wet and to listen – to hear if this time, any other of my kind heard me.

Red Light, Green Light

Just slightly off town center, facing the four corners, BJ sat on the first tier of the memorial to civil war veterans, directly beneath the words, "To those who shall not return." He was about to try again to exert his mental control over the village's one traffic light. The hot summer silence was only occasionally disrupted by the whisper of a gentle breeze through the great trees around him. His sneakers and socks lay scattered a few feet away, smelly debris in the still green pond of uniform close-clipped municipal grass that he so hated. "Give me weeds any day," he would grumble. "Who are you trying to impress, The Goddess of Golf?"

BJ's bare feet were pressed down before him. "Grounded in the Firmament," he would say. Both hands were raised touching his head. Little fingers met at the bridge of his nose, six digits pressed firmly to the forehead, a thumb at each temple. "Channeling the Chaos," he called it. Solemnly he announced aloud, "Fifth Effort."

Benjamin James Walker, Jr., the only son of the President of both the Rotary Club and the Chamber of Commerce, shut his eyes, lifted his shoulders, took a long slow deep breath, holding it, "Gathering the Force." The tip of his tongue protruded between his tight lips. In his mind he pictured the mechanism that made the light cycle. He had seen it the day before while the switches were serviced by the town electrician.

"Move," he mentally demanded, slowly exhaling. "MOVE!" The booming voice of an Olympian God roared in his head. "MOVE!" In his mind he saw the flare of lightning. He was sure the switch would shift, and the light would change from red to green. But, again, it remained red.

As if in answer to the sheer might of his effort, the clock on the Presbyterian church behind him began to chime. A log truck with a bad muffler blathered and backfired as it turned the

49

corner. In the distance the mid-afternoon freight train whistled its approach. BJ leapt to his feet, jumped up on the first tier of the memorial, threw his arms wide, and shouted to the world. "Is there no respect? This is Science happening here!" The red light continued to glare in his direction. BJ glared right back.

Behind him the church clock, heard from miles around, struck three. "Ha, Ha!" yelled BJ, jerking his right thumb back in umpire judgement. "Strike three, you're out!" He hopped down and went to retrieve his footwear.

Undaunted by another failure, but losing his interest in traffic control devices, BJ cheerfully sang to himself, "Cherry Coke, Cherry Coke, got to have a Cherry Coke," as he headed for Sydney's Luncheonette and Soda Fountain.

Exactly one-minute forty-five seconds after its last change, the traffic light, all on its own, turned green, just as it always did.

Hayin'–it

Seeing the heat waves shimmering over the river flats, smelling fresh cut alfalfa, hearing the buzz of insects punctuated by the distant roar of a diesel tractor, I am reminded of the summer the Four Horsemen of Hay came into being and got rich, which is also the same summer Vance nearly broke his leg, the same summer Benny found out he had to go to a private military academy, the same summer Dave got us guys fun and hard work together, and the same summer Mary Sue's shorts would not stay up. "Ooops," she would say to get us to look as she slowly pulled them back up from around her knees.

The four of us guys had been hanging around together after school all spring. As summer vacation began, we were together all day most days. We biked, talked, walked, fished, played baseball, and occasionally raised a little hell together. Most mornings I would skip out the door yelling back over my shoulder to mom, "Going out with the guys."

She would know I would most likely be with Dave from down the street. His dad ran the Feed Store and Mill in town. Dave had a slew of brothers and sisters, aunts and uncles, grandparents, and cousins all up and down the valley.

Probably Benny would show up. His dad was an undertaker with the business in his home. A lot of guys would not have anything to do with Benny since he lived with stiffs. But Dave and I thought he was funny, and Benny had important connections. He was friends with the town constable's oldest son. This kid was older than us and a loner who never hung out with us or anyone else. Benny could get him to steal confiscated fireworks from his father and get him to find out how to get into abandoned buildings downtown and other neat stuff of interest to young men looking for excitement in a small town.

If Benny was coming, then Vance would be there too. Vance lived next door to Benny down on East Main Street. He had only lived here a couple of years and was still trying to fit in. His dad was an engineer who worked in town at the secret defense plant, something to do with radar. Often the four of us could be found under one of the three bridges over Ramble Creek, trying to decide what to do for fun and adventure.

"Fishing? Fishing? You want to go fishing again? I'm sick of fishing." To emphasize the point, I threw a rock downstream, bouncing it off four boulders before it splashed into the water. Boulder skipping, we called it. "Four," I said.

"Yeah, but I can get my mom to make some baloney sandwiches," insisted Vance.

"Not with that yucky brown mustard again," said Dave making a face as he threw a rock hard. "Six," he said.

"We went fishing yesterday. You didn't catch anything did you Vance?" said Benny, carefully picking through the loose stones trying to find a really big rock.

"We could buy a watermelon and four bottles of soda and some potato chips and some marshmallows and play 'gotch-ya' up by the falls," pleaded Vance.

Struggling with a rock so large he could barely lift it, Benny said, "You offering to buy? I don't have any money."

"Me neither," said Dave throwing. "Five."

"Me neither," said I. "Four."

"Me neither," said Vance. "Darn. Two."

"Meteor!" yelled Benny, which was the signal for everyone to throw a rock into the nearest pool, making the biggest splash possible, getting us all soaked.

As we stood there dripping, Dave suddenly brightened saying, "My Dad says Mr. Benson needs some help getting his hay crop in and that he would hire all four of us."

"Yeah, how much would we make hayin'-it?" asked Benny.

"Five dollars a day and all the Kool-Aid we can drink," said Dave.

"Hey Vance," said Benny, "if you had five dollars, you could take Lydia to a movie and then I bet she'd go with you down to the river."

Ignoring Benny, Vance said, "I could get my mom to take us out there and come pick us up."

Early the next morning Vance's mom dropped the four of us off at the Benson Place. Dave, with farming family, was the only one with any idea what hayin'-it was, but we caught on. Old man Benson drove the tractor down neat rows of cut and raked hay, pulling along a big red baling machine which scooped up the dried grass in the front. Then it packed and compressed the hay in the middle and dropped regular twine-bound rectangular blocks of hay on the ground behind like a mechanical grasshopper laying eggs. We would follow along gathering the bales into piles of three or four so we would not have to carry them individually to the wagon.

After enough bales had been made to make two or three loads, Mr. Benson's mute hired hand, William, would drive a second tractor pulling a flat open wagon. It was our job to load it with the baled hay. We took turns who rode on the wagon and stacked the load because it was a lot easier than throwing the bales up from the ground. We learned the hard way, much to William's amusement, to cross pile the bales on the load so they would not fall off at the first bump.

It was Benny who invented the Four Horsemen of Hay. Each time we would finish loading a wagon, having stacked the bales as high as we dared, we would climb on top and strike a dramatic pose.

Benny would yell, "One for-all, and all for –" and we would shout in unison, "HAY!" as loud as we could, laugh, slap each other around and collapse to enjoy the ride. William would just shake his head as he drove us up to the barn.

We took turns unloading the bales onto a conveyer which carried the bales up and through a small opening in the upper level of the barn. In the hayloft we had to pack the bales tight because as we filled the barn, we had to walk on what we had just stacked. Vance made up "UNCLE," which meant stop sending in bales. The person unloading would try to make the three guys inside the barn yell "UNCLE" by sending in the hay so fast that the guys inside were in danger of getting buried.

After each load we would go to the milk house, which was cool and damp. Mrs. Benson would have a gallon of Kool-Aid floating in the refrigerated water-bath cooler the milk cans were kept in. We drank a gallon a load.

Mr. Benson worked at such a pace that soon there was no longer time to gather the bales before we threw them up on the wagon. When Dave started driving the tractor that was pulling the hay wagon, he would sometimes go so fast we had to run to keep up. Dave thought this was hysterical. Once, Vance was struggling to keep up, running with a bale across his chest. Suddenly he cried out in pain as he went to throw the bale. Instead of the hay bale going up into the wagon it stayed in one place and Vance went down into the ground. Just as he started to throw the bale, he had stepped into a big woodchuck hole. We stopped and ran to help. Benny and Dave each pulled on one of Vance's arms, and I dug around his leg to get him out. Just as we got him free old man Benson came up and said, "What happened?"

Vance said, "The Great God of Gophers grabbed me by the gonads." I did not think any of us were going to be able to breathe for laughing so hard. Thereafter, the Great God of Gophers was responsible for anything that went wrong.

As the hot sunny days passed, we filled that barn. We packed it, tight, right up to and including the peak. When we finished, we had three loads, with no place to put them, so we left them on the wagons. We felt like, and we knew, we had really done a piece of work. We were accomplished at hayin'-it. Mr.

Benson said to come by Saturday morning and he would pay us. He also said that the O'Neils up the road would like the Four Horsemen to come help put in their second crop of hay. I remember he said that Mrs. O'Neil put on a big feed at noon for the help every day, and not to miss it. Benny said, "They got any Kool-Aid?"

The next day Vance, Benny, and I were boulder skipping down under the bridge. Mary Sue was hanging around going "Ooops," every once in a while. Since she was two years younger than us, we pretended not to notice.

Vance was saying, "I'm going to buy a new fishing reel with my money. What are you going to do Benny?"

Dave came climbing down the bridge supports saying, "We can forget about the money from hayin'-it at the Benson farm. My Dad says the Benson barn burnt to the ground last night."

"Oh, God," Vance said.

We just sat there holding rocks in our hands when Benny finally said what we were all wondering. "Did we cause it?"

I said, "I don't know. It sure was hot in there yesterday and we filled it to the peak."

Dave said, "My Dad asked me if we filled it to the peak and was any of the hay wet?"

"How can it be wet and catch fire?" asked Benny.

The four of us walked out to the Benson Place. The barn, or what was left of it, was still smoldering. All that was left of the temple of our labors was the stone foundation, a few blackened beams, and the metal milk cooler which sat to the side on a concrete platform.

There was not a sign of the great work of the Four Horsemen. The Bensons were not around. With the neighbors we helped move the three loads of hay up the road to an empty barn on the next farm where the Benson's cows had already been taken.

During the rest of the summer, we were hayin'-it all up and down the valley. Always only if the farmer would hire all four of us. But there were no longer any Four Horsemen cheers or Gopher God catastrophes. Early in the fall we were asked to stop by the Grange Hall on Saturday morning. Mr. Benson was there. He thanked us and to our complete surprise he paid us. We saw Mary Sue as we left and I asked her if she had acquired a new belt or some suspenders, but she pretended not to hear me.

ABOUT THE AUTHOR

Craig Babcock began writing and sharing poems and short stories in high school. At one of the three colleges he attended he was there as a poet. In his last college he got into theatre and spent the next forty-three years performing and teaching as a solo mime and actor. When he retired from the stage, he overlapped into a second career as the Fire Marshal for a township in Northern New Jersey. He served for eleven years in that capacity – all this time creatively writing. It is a source of joy to Craig to turn out a well-expressed and well-received poem or short story. Enjoy!

Quantum is available at Lulu bookstore, lulu.com/shop.

www.ingramcontent.com/pod-product-compliance
Lightning Source LLC
Chambersburg PA
CBHW072339030726
47501CB00016BA/1707